The Lupie Warrior

By

Kristen Collins

Copyright © 2019 Kristen Collins

All rights reserved. No part of this publication may be reproduced, stored in a retrieval system, or transmitted, in any form or by any means mechanical, electronic, photocopying, recording or otherwise without the prior written consent of the publisher, nor be otherwise circulated in any form of binding or cover other than that in which it is published and without a similar condition being imposed on the subsequent purchaser.

Layout and design by No Sweat Graphics & Formatting
Editor: Suzette at My Write Hand VA

This book is a work of fiction. References to historical events, real people, or real locals are used fictitiously. Other names, characters, places and incidents are the product of the author's imagination, and any resemblance to actual events, locales or persons, living or dead, is entirely coincidental.

Printed in the United States of America

Always

K. Collins

Dedication

To all the Survivors of this invisible disease called Lupus, I dedicate this story to you. Fight on and never give up!

#Purple #LupieWarriors #LupusSucks

Lupus Foundation of America
https://www.lupus.org/

Acknowledgments

Samantha, I couldn't help but include you into my story as you have seen the disease I fight daily and are a true friend that sees me for me. I love you dearly.

Jon, my sweet and loving husband who has stuck by me since the beginning and continues to support me every day, even on the bad ones.

Always and Forever!

Chapter 1

You're stronger than you know, some say. Others say, you can do anything if you just believe in yourself. You can control your own fate and destiny, or so they say...

Well, they obviously have never battled Lupus, I thought as I sat inside my bubble that I called home once again. The same thing I have been doing daily since I was first diagnosed at the age of five.

I sat in my comfy window nook with my laptop opened and a book in my lap as I leaned back against the pillow wall. The window was open, and the wind blew across my face as I admired the thunderclouds that floated in the Texas sky. Lightning flashed and thunder rolled like music to my ears. I love storms; they brighten the mood of my mundane everyday life.

The video chat sounded and I rolled my eyes, annoyed by the disturbance, but tilted my head enough to see that my best friend, Samantha, was calling.

I wasn't in the mood to talk but then again, I never was. If I could, I would never deal with the outside world again. However if I don't answer, Samantha will be beating my door down within the hour.

Reluctantly, I answered anyway, "Good morning, Samantha."

"My, don't *you* sound extra perky this morning. Are you at home working?" She said sarcastically.

"You know me, always around. I mean, where can I go?" I said, rolling my eyes.

"To Joe's Bar with me tonight for a speed dating event..." she said nonchalantly.

I buried my face under my arm and pleaded with my crazy best friend.

"No, no, no, Samantha. You *know* how my Lupus symptoms flare up at random and how bad the last one went. Emo guy... *Remember*?!" I moaned.

At the horrible memory, I burst out laughing as my hands covered my face.

"Ooh Kristen, he *was* pretty bad, but you were not the only one who suffered that night, every girl had to deal with him and his painted white face with black lips! Do you remember how..." she cracked up, unable to finish.

"Yeah, exactly!" I said pointing at her knowingly. "I thought I was on a date with an ugly, scrawny, wannabe-version of the wrestler, Sting!"

"Okay, I promise this time I will do something about it instead of sitting there laughing the entire time. I'll buy you wings, okay?" she teased.

"Well, it would be an injustice to turn down some good wings. Taste is about the one thing Lupus doesn't affect badly."

"How are you feeling today, Kristen?" Samantha asked sympathetically.

"It's a cloudy day, so I feel pretty good actually. I'll take a nap after lunch, that way I should feel good tonight. I have some graphic design work to do today that will keep me from worrying about the speed dating event at Uncle Joe's bar the rest of the time."

"What are you working on? Is it another author's book cover or some marketing for another business?"

"Another cover for Sky Collins' newest book! Which means I need to go if I am going to be ready on time for tonight."

"Ugh, fine," she groaned dramatically. "Oh, and one more thing, Kris."

"Hmm? What's that?" I asked.

"Wear your cutest boots and jean skirt," she winked.

I laughed, going along with her comment about what to wear, "Sure thing, Samantha. See ya this evening to get ready."

"Love ya!" she smiled mischievously.

I shook my head, "Love ya too."

I rolled back onto my fluffy pillows and smiled thinking about Uncle Joe. I love my uncle dearly. He has taken care of me since I was abandoned at the fire station in our small town. Joe was a firefighter back then but when he retired, he opened a bar of his own in our small town.

He raised me as a single father, my adoptive father, but never made me call him dad but rather Uncle Joe. When I asked him why one time, I remember him saying; "I wish I was but I'm just filling in for the parents who couldn't take care of you."

Part of me always wondered if he secretly knew my parents but honestly I just didn't care. I was one of the lucky ones. Most orphans grew up and went into a crazy search for their birth parents but not me. Uncle Joe was the most relaxed parent ever and the bond of trust between us was strong. Unfortunately, I was always sick. As a little girl, I loved playing out in the sun every day. The weather didn't matter, I was always out in it.

Then one day, my life was changed forever. I woke up from naptime one day at school covered from head to toe in red itchy bumps that turned purplish after a few days before fading away. The kids were cruel and ran away from me screaming *eww!* and *Freak!*

The teacher called my Uncle Joe and he immediately took me to the Emergency Room, but what they thought was just poison ivy from recess turned into something much worse.

After months of endless doctor visits, and multiple painful and excruciating tests and medicines that never helped any of my symptoms, we finally received a diagnosis. I was allergic to the sun but, upon further testing, a new invisible disease was to actually be blamed. While I was still allergic to the sun, I was also diagnosed with Lupus. Most people who have Lupus usually have one or the other, whether that be systemic or discoid, but of course I was the lucky ten percent that had both.

From that point on, I would forever be annoyed with permanent long sleeve tops, pants, and wide brim hats for extra shading to cover my face. I could no longer go outside between certain times for my health's sake and I would have to wear masks in certain areas.

If I caught the flu or even a simple cold then it would take me twice as long to recover from it. Most of the time, I would have to make a trip to the hospital because the antibiotics weren't enough to fight the illnesses.

After I was diagnosed, the kids at school began to distance themselves from me, which meant I never fit in with any particular group of kids, and so the bullying started. With one incident and multiple doctor visits, I had become an outsider. Kids can be cruel to one another but it is the way of growing up, I thought... That's not me excusing their awful behavior but instead of letting it get to me, I built myself up from it.

One fateful day there was a new girl, Samantha, who transferred into our small town from the big city and on that day, everything changed for me. We were instant friends and whenever someone tried to bully me, Samantha was right there to take up for me.

Uncle Joe loved Samantha as much as I did, and he was always our advocate whenever we were in trouble in the principal's office. Every time I ended up in the hospital, Samantha found a way to be by my side as much as possible.

She spent her weekends inside with me, and helped me be outside in ways Uncle Joe and I could never have figured out. Somehow, her extroverted personality meshed well with my introverted one.

Samantha was like my sister even though we didn't share any blood relation between us; no, the bond went deeper than that…we were soul sisters and it's a bond I would never forsake, no matter what.

Chapter 2

The morning passed with the same amount of entertainment as my daily life...meaning none. I put together the romance cover for my author client, Sky Collins. Her books were my escape from the harsh realities I faced daily.

I laid back, swearing that I would only rest my eyes for a few minutes, but the banging on the door woke me from a sleepy stupor. I rolled over, ignoring it, but a bubbly voice refused to let me go back to LaLa land.

"Kristen, get up. It's time to get ready," Samantha said, shaking me.

I moaned and covered my head. "Noooo... The pillow is begging me to stay," I whined.

"Ooh, I bet it is. Too bad you're cheating on it tonight with food and music," she laughed as she yanked the covers off me.

"What time is it?!" I asked, confused.

"It's five o'clock. You'll feel better once you shower, I'll wait for you in the living room," she said as she skipped off happily.

"You make me want to hate you," I mumbled.

"But you can't. You love me!" she sang back. I rolled my eyes at her super hearing and stuck my tongue out like a child.

"You roll those eyes at me again, and I'm going to pop them out next time," she said, popping her head back into my room.

"Wha... I would never!" I feigned innocence, horribly.

"We're best friends, I know your moodiness better than you," she joked as she waved her finger at me.

"Fine, I'm up! I'll be ready quickly," I said, as I struggled to get out of bed.

My feet stung as if I was standing on needles, which indicated swelling but I went off to the bathroom to enjoy a thoroughly hot shower.

After about twenty minutes, I was out and dolled up. Before stumbling out of the bathroom, I opened my mirror to the mounds of medicine bottles and began taking the countless meds that would help me survive another day. My least favorite method of staying alive. I cringed as I pulled the syringe from the shelf, injecting the cool liquid into my hip. You would think I would be used to the injections by now but my hips still screamed at me daily from it.

Briefly, I paused before I strolled into the living room feeling like new – for the moment anyway —and did a model spin for Samantha. I adjusted my off-the-shoulder top and played with the fringes around the bottom. My leather belt sparkled in the light.

"Ooo... Cute outfit. I love your round-toed, double stitched boots. Are those the ones with the cross design stitched on the side?" she asked as she beamed with excitement.

"Yes, they are!" I said, excitedly. "Let's go before I start feeling like crap!"

"You got it, Hoss!" Samantha said, jumping up from the couch, beating me to the door.

We drove across the bridge, through the small town and landed at Joe's bar. The car ride was fast in Samantha's VW Beetle truck and the fresh air was invigorating. Reaching for the saloon doors, I pulled them open as wide as possible for us as I quickly made my way through the crowded bar to gather some liquid courage for Samantha and me.

Samantha was hot on my tail, as she fanned herself looking around. I was already feeling the light fever coming on as the moon was coming up in the evening Texas sky. An unfortunate part of my invisible disease was unexplained fevers, aches, and chills. My body will be as hot as a sauna, but I'll feel cold on the inside. Sometimes my fingertips and toes turn blue and get as cold as ice. Then there are the lovely blisters and butterfly rash across my face, from cheek to cheek, that pop up unexpectedly.

Feeling *good* or having a *good* day is not a real thing, it's truly a minute by minute way of life. One minute, I could be feeling incredible and the very next it could be very intense nerve pain that seems like it will never end, yet only lasts a few seconds. With an invisible disease comes chaos in its unpredictability and intensity.

To say I have missed out on a lot of life experiences is an understatement. Eventually, I stopped going to outings because I would end up overdoing it by either being in the sun one minute too long or I ate or drank something that I shouldn't have.

"Looks like a full crowd," Samantha said matter-of-factly, turning towards the bar.

We both smiled as my Uncle Joe, owner of this clean and great bar in our small town, came up to us to get us some drinks.

"Hey, Uncle Joe," we both said, leaning over, kissing him on both cheeks.

"Hey, girls. Y'all look nice tonight, hoping to luck out and meet your soul mates?" He teased, wiggling his eyebrows, causing us to burst out laughing. He popped the caps on two Mike's Hard Lemonades, our favorites, then poured us three shots of tequila as well.

"Uncle Joe, you know that love at first sight is for the birds," I exclaimed as we grabbed the shots and clinked the glasses together.

"Cheers to a great and safe night. May the angel of love bless us tonight!" Samantha said, full of giddiness. I rolled my eyes at my optimistic friend and my Uncle Joe just chuckled at us.

"Look girls, this event turned out to be bigger than I thought it would be. There's a bunch of out-of-towners that I don't recognize here. If any of them get crazy with you and make you uncomfortable, just brush your shoulder and I'll grab Heifer here and take care of them," he said as he picked up his wooden bat engraved with 'Heifer' across it and patted it into his hand.

"Sure thing, Unc. We promise not to get into any trouble," I said with a wink.

I took a snickering Samantha's hand and pulled her away from the bar and across the room to our spot by each other, the little two-person tables made a huge horseshoe on the backside of the building. We watched as the DJ prepped his booth while the waitress, Bridget, walked from table to table, placing beautiful masks on them. I reached out, gently squeezing Bridget's arm as she passed us.

"What's all the masks for tonight?" I giggled.

"Ooh, didn't Samantha tell you that the event is masquerade themed tonight? That way, it makes it more interesting," she said, with a wink as she dashed off, dropping more masks onto the remaining tables.

My heart dropped at the thought of the exhaustion level, and the ultimate toll it would take on me before the night was over. Especially when the morning comes, I will be sick for days! Maybe I should leave and just call it a night. I followed Samantha and was about to chastise her when a buzz went out around the DJ booth.

Uncle Joe was handed a microphone. "Good evening, everyone. I am pleased to have you all join us tonight for the first masquerade speed-date event at Joe's Bar. I want everyone to have a good time tonight. I only have one rule. Men, do not, under any circumstances, get creepy or rude with the ladies, and women, do not go psycho on the men, or I will throw you out of my bar. If you find someone you don't want to let go, hit the buzzer in the middle of your table. Good luck and I wish you all a successful night."

I smiled as the now older hefty man, whom I loved as dearly as a father figure, walked off the stage and perched himself behind the bar to serve drinks and keep an eye on everyone.

My eyes drifted back to the line of men who walked to each table, all ranges of sizes; tall, short, big, lanky, and deathly skinny… my nerves rattled from previous experience. I don't judge men typically by appearance but if a man has more eyeliner on than me, then Houston, we have a serious problem.

The DJ wrapped his beat headphones around his neck as he said, "All right, all right, all right y'all. You know the drill, you have ten minutes to meet your mystery date, but if that special someone slips into your bubble, don't be afraid to hit that buzzer. On my mark…" He lifted a mini foghorn and sounded it, "Go!"

Immediately, a burly redneck sat across from me. His Confederate flag tattoo covered his triceps, scissors had cut off his sleeves and frayed pieces of strings remained. I examined what I could see of his face, but the dip in his mouth instinctively made me want to gag as specks of it covered his tobacco-stained teeth.

Samantha and I sideways glanced at each other as I smiled sweetly at him and held out my hand.

"Hi, I'm Kristen."

"Well, sweet cheeks. I'm Cleetus."

"So tell me about yourself, Cleetus," I said, mustering up as much courage as possible for the next ten minutes of my life.

He leaned in towards me. "How about me and you get out of this joint?"

"Excuse me?" I said sitting back, not knowing whether to feel appalled or disgusted by his gesture. Who am I kidding? It was definitely both.

"I said, how about we take this back to my place and pick up this conversation in a much more comfortable setting..."

"Umm... I think I'm good. Next!" I yelled, catching everybody's attention.

"Next? You're *nexting* me?!" he said, raising his voice.

I was taken back by his tone, I knew I had insulted him but let's face it. He was a creep. He should have taken the hint and just moved on but from the looks of this, it was about to get ugly and quick.

"Hey, hick! I think that's enough," Samantha started to stand, ready to come to my defense.

I quickly beat her to the punch. I was a woman, yes. I had an immune disease, yes. But I was *not* weak. "Yes, *next*. Now leave before I have you thrown out," I snarled at him.

"You high-class skank. You think you're better than me, don't you?" he spat, reaching across the table, grabbing my arm.

I was about to yell for the bouncers when a tall, broad man grabbed his shoulder. Cleetus quickly released my arm but I could feel a bruise from his grip under the skin as I rubbed my arm in an effort to ease the pain.

His eyes were an onyx color and his five o'clock shadow definitely piqued my interest, especially his build. His suit pants hugged his hips in all the right places, snug on the hips and loose fitting the rest of the way down. They were one of those expensive ones, specially tailored. My eyes wandered upwards, loving his tightly fitting jacket. The man was fit, and my hands itched to touch him.

I didn't have time to admire him anymore as he took the situation I was in into his own hands.

"I think the lady has asked you to leave nicely and more than once," he stated bluntly.

"Who the hell do you think you are, city slicker? Get your hands off me," Cleetus said aggressively.

The obnoxious redneck threw his right fist, about to strike the stranger when the guy grabbed his fist mid-air. I gasped in shock as did most of the now watching room. He grabbed Cleetus by the collar, pulling him slightly off the ground.

I swear, for the briefest of moments, his eyes flashed a strange amber color. His demeanor screamed boss man, the alpha dog.

"I will not repeat myself again. The lady asked you to leave and you will do it *now*. Am I understood?" he said, his tone deathly.

Cleetus shoved himself away from the stranger, "Yeah. Whatever, you're both crazy. I'm out of here." He stormed off out of the bar, and out of sight.

I exhaled a breath I didn't realize I was holding and stared down at the table.

Samantha reached over and squeezed my shoulder. "Are you okay, Kris?"

I saw my hands trembling while they sat on the table and quickly hid them under it. "Yeah, I'm fine," I said with the best bravado I could muster.

I watched out of my periphery as Uncle Joe was coming from around the bar with Heifer in his hands. I shook my head at him and held my trembling hand out to show him to stop and leave it be. Uncle Joe and some bouncers took off out of the bar, probably to find the creep and threaten him or something fatherly-like. Uncle was a bit on the hefty side, so he didn't move like he used to in his younger days. He was still a great bodyguard though and a loving father figure in my life.

"Excuse me, Miss," the stranger said. "Are you okay?"

I stared at him, slightly mesmerized, lost in the depths of his jeweled eyes barreling deep into mine.

"Miss?"

"What? Oh yes, I'm fine. Thank you so much for that."

A buzzer rang, and the bell sounded, signaling that one person had met 'the one' – well for the night most likely – and for the rest to move onto the next person.

The guy across from Samantha stood and moved towards me but the stranger gave him one look and said, "Not this one, buddy, move on," he commanded. The guy ducked his head and nodded, moving on. The guy didn't even put up a fight as he walked off.

I chuckled. The guy was a pushover, which would have made me "next" him anyway. Mr. Mysterious Stranger just showed me all of that more quickly than ten minutes.

"May I sit here, Ma'am?" he asked softly.

"Yes, by all means, please do," I said with a genuine smile this time, gesturing with my hand towards the chair.

I reached out my hand to him, "I'm Kristen and a local. But judging by your suit, and based on the fact that I know just about everybody that lives in this town, you, Sir, are new to this small town," I said matter-of-factly.

I admired his suit; it was different and nice all at the same time. I wondered if it was specially tailored to him specifically because it fit him like a glove. Also, the charcoal color did wonders to bring out his onyx colored eyes.

He chuckled deeply, "Very observant, Kristen. Yes, I am and my name is Derek."

"So what brings you to Llano of all places, Derek? I know no one goes out of their way to just show up to some speed dating event, in the middle of Nowheresville," I laughed.

"You're right, I'm just passing through and thought I would stop in for a drink and to spend the night. You see, I'm a businessman and have been traveling all day from Dallas to Austin and then tomorrow, I will be heading to the mountains of Colorado. I just couldn't resist stopping and sightseeing some of the rest of Texas," he explained with a half-smile.

"Wow," I said genuinely interested for once. "So, what is it that you do, Mr. Businessman," I teased.

The vibes I felt were nothing like I had ever experienced before. This man was different. Staring him in the eyes, I felt a strange feeling to look away; maybe it was because he seemed very assertive, like he held authority. He just seemed so... mysterious. That didn't seem like the right word... Was it the unknown or maybe it was forbidden? Yes, that was the word. Forbidden. But I liked it. I liked it a lot...

"I'm in the alcohol business, it's actually a family business. My family makes moonshine," he said and his smile broadened at the dumbfounded look on my face.

Dumbfounded, yes. However, I was more impressed by him and his family business than anything else. Colorado was an economic boomer with the now legal pot industry over there.

"Wait a minute. I'm going to call your bluff. Everyone knows moonshine is illegal."

Derek chuckled at me, "Yes but mine, on the other hand, is very legal and approved. In fact, I just picked up a customer here. The owner of this bar has very enthusiastically agreed to sell my family's product."

"Uncle Joe did, huh? Yup, he's never one to turn down an exciting business opportunity." I smiled over at the middle-aged man I love. For a brief moment, I watched him as he pulled chilled mugs out of the freezer and poured drafts to perfection for the thirsty patrons eagerly waiting.

"I'm such a nut. I never would have guessed that you two were family," he said, surprised and shook his head. "But this is a small town, I should have known better."

I giggled at his naivety, "It's okay. You're not from here, but he is my uncle *and* a great man."

"So what do you do, Kristen?" he asked curiously.

"I'm a graphic designer. I design book covers, logos, business cards and such, for people. I promote my little business online for a little expansion." My stomach twisted into knots at the thought of being honest with Derek. Even though we'd just met, I didn't want to scare him off. But lying to him just didn't sit well with me, and the thought actually made me nauseous.

Sitting up a little straighter in my chair, I pulled the courage from thin air. "I'm not going to lie; I'm a homebody, Netflix and chill-type gal. What about you?"

The knot of fear in my stomach twisted tighter as I waited for him to ask more inquisitive questions. How would he react then? Just like all the rest? Leave and never be heard from again like most of the people in my life, with the exception of Samantha and Uncle Joe that is.

"A homebody, huh. Why's that?" he asked, but before I could answer, the ten-minute buzzer sounded. I had no chance to react before Derek hit the buzzer in the middle of the table.

To say that I was stunned by Derek's action was an understatement. The fear knotting in my stomach turned into butterflies of excitement. He chose me?

Samantha squealed beside me in excitement and squeezed my shoulder encouragingly. She leaned over and hugged me as she whispered into my ear, "Would you pick up your jaw and give the knight in shining armor a chance!" she whispered, chastising me lovingly.

I nodded and took a deep breath as I held my chin high. I knew he had been watching mine and Samantha's little interaction before I had turned back around because I could see him out of the corner of my eye as he leaned back in his chair smiling.

"Friend?" he asked.

My smile widened, "Yes, my best friend, actually."

I picked up my drink, sipping it, as I glanced back at her, only to see her watching us intently, as if we were a dramatic TV show she couldn't get enough of. Samantha mouthed, *don't screw this up!*

He chuckled as I coughed and my drink halfway spewed out at Samantha. I rolled my eyes.

"You okay?" he asked.

"Yes," I answered quickly and changed the subject. My cheeks heated with embarrassment as I took the napkin he handed me and I patted the liquid off my clothing. "You know, it's supposed to be women's choice picking," I said, lifting an eyebrow.

Derek laughed and shrugged at me as he leaned over the table, "I find you very intriguing, Kristen, and I'm not ready to let you go just yet," he winked flirtatiously at me.

I giggled as I shook my head in disbelief at him. Again, I found myself surprised by him, and the battle inside raged on between two sides of me. Should I let this stranger in or should I keep up the wall I worked so hard to build up for so long?

Derek's voice brought me out of my thoughts.

"You haven't answered my question yet. Why?" he said, as he gazed intently into my eyes. I had to sit back and look away from his intense gaze, although I felt excited by catching his interest.

"I have a better idea. Can you dance?" I asked playfully. Changing the topic was the best I could offer him at the moment. His questions prodded at my vulnerability, and I wasn't quite sure I liked it yet. I found him enticing, and frightening...not a scary I'm-afraid-of-you frightening, but a deeper, unexplainable frightening. Maybe it was the fear of the unknown? I would chew on it later after the night was over.

I'd caught him off guard apparently as he warily said, "Yes..."

I downed the rest of my drink using the liquid courage to my benefit for once. I knew I would regret drinking later, but tonight I wanted more out of life than the boring routine I had to endure daily. Lupus had robbed my life of so much that tonight I decided

I would be in charge of my own fate and destiny, just for once.

Using my two fingers and pursing my lips, I whistled for Uncle Joe's attention and gave him the thumbs up. Joe signaled the DJ and he did a funk, like a record was skipping.

"Ladies and gentlemen! Please take your positions on the dance floor," The DJ announced. Only the locals knew what was going on which made Samantha and I giggled anxiously.

Samantha jumped up out of her seat yelling, "Ah heck, yeah! Finally! Come on, Sugar!" as she grabbed the handsome guy's hand she was talking with.

The music picked up as we walked onto the dance floor, the sound of a seductive honkytonk tango mix came through the speakers, and the tango beat made my legs walk with purpose. A man that can dance such a passionate dance gets a huge vote in my book on any day.

The women lined up next to each other. Samantha, always the faithful friend, stood next to me as the men lined up across from us. The DJ spun the record to remix it, starting the song over. Samantha and I smiled at the confused looks on some of the guests' faces but once the song started over, we walked towards our partners and I couldn't resist staring into his eyes. It was invigorating, and it could have been the alcohol but I felt amazing and numb to my Lupus. The thoughts of my disease were in the back of my mind locked away, just for the night.

Our eyes locked with one another and the rest of the room disappeared. I stalked towards him, placing a hand on his tight chest; he was muscular, and those thoughts made chills crawl up my back. I stepped backwards, feeling like prey caught in the predator's eyesight.

It was a strange yet enticing feeling, a powerful feeling that bloomed from within me. In my life, every day, I was a powerless victim to my disease and it bullied and victimized me every second, taking the most precious things I could afford. Robbing me like a mugger in an alleyway on the streets of New York. In these fleeting moments of life, I don't often get to feel this addicting power that women held, a power that comes from the soul of every fighter.

He grabbed my hand and brushed his lips softly across my knuckles as we bowed to each other, as was the manner to start the famous tango dance. We circled one another in the ritualistic way as we came together full circle and Derek wrapped his arm around my waist. I placed my hand on his shoulder as our free hands locked together.

The tango has been called the "Dance of Sorrow" as it represented frustrated love and human fatality, although originally the dance was not so deep and serious.

Our feet slid across the floor as our heads looked away from one another. A small voice in my conscience whispered, *hurry and walk away; you could never be enough for someone like him. He'll leave you once he finds out what's wrong with you. You're weak and pathetic.* I avoided eye contact as I let the inner voice win, it was right, but I didn't want to leave. The struggle inside grew as I fought between rational and irrational feelings. Derek was strong as he guided me and, as I stepped my left foot over right as if I couldn't figure out if I wanted to run away or stay in his arms, I turned to walk away but Derek's strong arms grabbed my elbows, pulling me back and spinning me back to him.

For a split second, it seemed as if time froze and it was just Derek and I in that moment. Maybe it was the sense of authority the air held around him. I got the feeling that most people (women especially) didn't turn him down or away very often. There was something else I couldn't put my finger on quite yet. How could a man make me feel both cowardly and courageous at the same time? What was he not saying that made my intuition scream out, *pay attention, you twit!*

With the ease of a professional, he dipped me backwards as he pulled my thigh up to him. Derek pulled me up, making my heart flutter as he spun me, bringing me back and we slid one leg backwards, pulling us apart and low to the ground but back up. We were both spinning together in a circle, pivoting on one foot with our legs between the others. He spun me out away from him and my heart raced as he spun me back to him into his arms.

Effectively, Derek worked his way to where we were dancing backwards, side by side. He pulled me back to him as he dipped me, swaying me from left to right as he firmly pulled me up to his chest, grabbing my thigh and pulling my leg up, just as the song ended.

Our faces were barely inches apart from one another, leaving me breathless. Who was this mysterious man before me? His eyes were full of promises, promises he couldn't possibly keep. Or could he? I was lost in his eyes, the wave of onyx and the depths ate my soul up from the inside out. For a moment, I was lost in the bliss and the freedom from the illness that often controlled my human life. Death was no longer the warden that once held the chains that kept me prisoner.

"You want to get out of here?" he asked.

I looked over at Samantha as she stared wide-eyed. She mouthed, *Yes!* at me as I looked back at Derek and whispered, "Yes, I do..."

Chapter 3

The night air was warm and welcoming as we walked outside of the bar. Derek started heading to his '67 Mustang as my mouth dropped open in envy.

"Is that your car?!" I exclaimed with excitement.

Derek's smile broadened as he said, "Yeah, she's been in the family for years, passed down from my Grandpappy to my dad, then to me,"

He ran his hand over the hood of the classic as we both admired it. The Mustang was cherry red with black racing stripes through the middle from the front to the back.

"You want to ride in her?" he asked.

"Well, does a pig like slop?!" Derek's face held bewilderment to it, so I quickly added, "Never mind, and don't answer that. But yes, I would really enjoy that a lot," I said, jumping up and down with enthusiasm.

He walked over and opened the passenger door for me. "After you."

I did a fake bow as we both laughed and I hopped into his car and relaxed instantly in the black leather seats. Derek smiled with elation as he jumped in and started the engine. The car purred calmly and I couldn't contain the anticipation that threatened to bubble over. Derek pulled out and started cruising through town as I pointed the way to a back road; he took my direction eagerly.

"You can't get lost on the back roads, they all eventually lead to somewhere, mostly another town or back to here."

"You're the navigator, now what do you want to do?"

Feeling wild and free, I decided to live carefree and in the moment. If I'm going to die eventually from this disease then I wanted to go out with wonderful memories to take with me.

"Derek, drive like hell is chasing you," I said, feeling like someone else. Someone who wasn't sick 24/7, like the girl I could be without Lupus ruling every moment of my life.

"Yes, ma'am."

Derek took the turns on the dirt road with precision like he was a professional driver. I whooped and hollered out the window. The speed felt exhilarating and I couldn't get enough, or maybe the alcohol in my system was doing all the talking for me. He pulled up to an old concrete road that went through the middle of a small river crossing. Instead of building a bridge back in the day, they dammed up the water and built this concrete road. There are gaps under the road that allows the fish and water to pass through. Derek put the car in park as he turned off the engine.

"This is what we call The Slab. The locals know this spot very well and come here more than the regular spots on the river that the tourists visit. Every once in a while a tourist will find this gem to enjoy on a hot day. It's a really popular spot for the local teenagers, more so at night, ya know, parties and all," I said excitedly.

He turned to me but I hopped out of the car instead, I couldn't stop the playful behavior that had gotten into me. I giggled as I threw my shoes off and headed towards the water bank. I heard Derek get out of the car and follow me, he joined me in no time at all.

"Isn't the full moon, and these stars in the night sky, just the most beautiful thing you have ever seen?" I said absentmindedly.

"Colorado skies *are* beautiful but I have to say Texas ones are right up there in the top five list with them. You know, you are not like any woman I have ever met, Kristen," he said as he stared at me.

"I bet you tell all the girls that, Derek," I teased.

"Nah, I prefer honesty. Most women I have met are high maintenance and I like those who live a simple life. Someone who wants me for me and not my money."

"Hmm, that must be very lonely to have to live with," I said sympathetically.

"What are you not telling me, Kristen? I asked you a question back at the bar and you dodged it, very well I might add, with a superb distraction that I certainly wouldn't mind doing again with you," he said, with a mischievous glint in his eyes.

I stiffened at his reminder of the question I was trying so hard to dodge. The same old thoughts and fears came back like a bad nightmare I couldn't shake. I wanted so desperately to just escape it all that I felt more drawn to be wild and carefree than I should allow myself.

He took my hand that was playing with the sand. I let him, and I could feel the electric current from his touch throughout my body. Needless to say, this man and everything about him turned me on. A pang of sadness washed over me at the thought that this wouldn't last. But another part of me asked, *why not? Why does it have to end?*

"If I tell you every little detail about me, then this night will end a lot sooner. Although, this... it would have never lasted past tonight anyways. If I took you back to my place or to your hotel...Well, you would have snuck out in the early morning rays, never to be heard from again," I said, not looking at him, *dang, could I ruin a mood or what...*

"Kristen, I don't know what kind of men you're used to, but I don't just use women and walk away. That's not in me; I don't use women because I respect them too much. I know I barely know you, but you seem like a great person. I would like to get to know you more. I swear, whatever it is, it won't make me run away," he said sincerely.

I took a deep breath. Might as well rip the band aid right off. "Derek, I'm sick."

"Oh, I can take you home if you're not feeling well, Kristen," he said, starting to get up but I tugged him back down and shook my head.

"No, Derek, I don't mean from a cold or the alcohol, although, I will probably regret it tomorrow. I mean like I'm *sick*," I said quietly and stared at him, waiting for the lightbulb to come on.

"Like cancer? Do you have cancer, Kristen?" he said seriously. His brows furrowed with worry and my heart sank. I've seen that look before. I didn't know him, but like every time before when I saw that look, my heart broke and sadness threatened to eat me alive. I wanted to curl up into my ball and hide away from the world once again. This is why I don't date or go out because I am just setting myself up for pain, not the physical kind that Lupus brings, but the emotional kind that can bring the bravest down to their knees.

I gave a short laugh, "No, not cancer but have you ever heard of Lupus?"

"Maybe once or twice but I don't recall what that is really."

"It's an autoimmune disease, where my body basically attacks itself. I haven't been able to *really* go outside my whole life. I sit inside where it's safe and hide from the direct sunlight. All my windows are tinted in my house to protect me because my skin will blister up, so I watch the world from the safety of my home. I enjoy cloudy days because they're safer, and I go out at night for any kind of fun. I've never been to the beach, and I have to wear long sleeves, pants and a huge, silly looking hat to go to the doctors.

Other than that, I would never venture outside before the sun was setting. Oh, if I catch a cold or the flu then it takes me twice as long as a normal person to recover. Most of the time, I end up in the hospital before it gets any better," I said with resentment deep in my voice.

I could feel the bitterness and anger rising inside as I frowned, looking away as I revealed my secret that only a few knew. Waiting for the inevitability of the secret I held coming out, ruining the moment between us.

"Kristen I could never imagine having to live like that or what you must have to go through on a daily basis. That just makes me admire you even more," he said with a smile that seemed genuine, if a little sad.

God, his smile was gorgeous; I wanted to kiss his full lips, just to taste them.

"Admire me? There is nothing to admire about me, Derek," I said nonchalantly.

He turned to me and his fingers caressed my chin, turning my face towards him.

"Did I say admire? That wasn't the right word. I marvel at the depth of your resolve because you are a fighter, you refuse to let this disease take you from this world without a fight," he said with what felt like pride.

"The problem is, people do not understand that I am doing what I have to do to live my life on the best terms possible and they would do the same, given my set of circumstances. Yes, it's hard. Yes, I'd like it to be different and easier. What they're implying is secretly screaming in the back of my head, *'I'm sorry it's you but I'm glad it's not me because I couldn't live like that.'* It's almost like pity disguised as puffed up groundless admiration."

Derek leaned in closer, just a breath away as he whispered, "Believe me, nothing about what I am feeling has even a hint of pity."

My heart pounded in my chest, part of me felt like he could hear it. Heck, I could hear and feel it both. Once again, my milk chocolate-ty eyes locked with his jeweled onyx ones, and his gaze was too intense for me. I had to look away, I felt like his eyes were reading my soul and he was unlocking all the secrets about me.

My smile returned, and I felt safe with him, this handsome and kind stranger. I suddenly had an idea. "Would you like to go for a swim?"

He didn't answer and for a moment, the self-doubt that ruled my mind made me wonder if I'd ruined things, but instead he got up and started stripping his clothes off so I did the same. The night was full of surprises as it seemed nothing could scare Derek away or turn the night into any of the disastrous bad dates I have had in the past. I reveled in it.

I would take whatever happiness I could get in what would eventually be a short life for me. Most likely, as it is with most people who suffer from Lupus, I would die of organ failure before I even hit my seventies. Being on such a large amount of intensive medication is essentially a catch- 22 in the end. While they all help keep me alive, they can also wear down my organs that process them a lot faster. People like me don't have the luxury of a long life.

I sent up a prayer of thanks for the cover of darkness so that he couldn't see all the scars I carried from surgeries and more. But Derek gasped behind me as I turned and saw him looking at me.

"What happened to your body, Kristen?" he asked as he ran his hand over the scars all over my body, some on my stomach and others on my back and arms.

Self-consciously I pulled away, "Wow, that's some vision you have there. They're scars from past surgeries and other things," I said, with an uneasiness in my voice.

I felt more vulnerable at the fact that as he could see my body when I thought I'd be hidden, it seemed like what I hid most in my soul was vividly apparent as well. His unusual vision was eerie, but I chalked it up to the moonlight shining down on us.

I turned and ran to a rock and dove into the deep water. Running from Derek and his endless curiosity, running from the scars on my body, from the Lupus that haunted and dictated everything in my life. As soon as I came up from the depths of the warm water, Derek was coming up behind me.

He wrapped his arms around my waist as we floated back towards the shallower parts of the water. He ran his nose up and down my neck and left a trail of soft kisses, heat was left in their place. I couldn't help the whispered moans that escaped my lips.

I turned around in his arms and wrapped mine around his neck as I did the same with my legs around his waist. He tightened his embrace as his left hand wrapped around the back of my neck, massaging it as he leaned in and we kissed. My head fell to the side as his lips ran down my neck, his teeth nipped and teased the soft skin, but the gesture just drove me even more wild.

I tightened my legs around his waist, pulling me closer to him. At that moment, I realized that he wasn't wearing any pants at all. His hand ran down my back and I felt the material being ripped away. I felt him bite that all so sensitive spot between my shoulder and neck but it only hurt a second, then I felt a euphoric sensation running through my veins from head to toe.

He closed the distance and I opened myself to him. I was adrift in his presence and the want. He was touching a part of me that had never been released. It was like a part of me had been caged and locked away until that moment in time and he released me, showing me freedom I never knew I didn't have.

The feeling of his touch and motions were sensational as stars covered my vision. We were both lost in a tangle of each other as he guided me towards the sandy bank and laid me back. His kisses trailed over me as we found the release we were both longing for between one another.

He pulled me gently out into the water, just deep enough for him to sit in. I turned and sat in his lap, leaning back as we both gazed at the stars. Neither one of us spoke for a while but revelled in one another's embrace.

Over the next few hours, we talked about our families and our lives. I poured out everything to Derek, my hopes, my dreams, and deepest wishes that would never come true.

Chapter 4

Once we finally left the comfort of the warm water, I followed Derek to the back of his car as he popped the trunk. He dug through his suitcase, grabbing a few towels and some clothes. He handed me a pair of sweats and one of his cotton t-shirts.

"My clothes are dry, they didn't get wet." I said, confused.

Derek walked over to the shoreline where my clothes sat piled and kicked them into the water.

"Oops. I thought that was a rock," he shrugged and smiled mischievously.

I walked over to where he was standing, dumbfounded that he just kicked my clothes into the water but I couldn't contain the laughter that bubbled up through me.

"Uh huh... Sure ya did. Just one favor..." I said snuggled up to his chest and wrapped my hands around his towel that sat around his waist.

"Anything. Name it," he whispered, his eyes shut as he leaned into me and I swore I heard him growl under his breath..

"Be a doll and grab my clothes that are floating away."

Derek's eyes popped open just in time as I grabbed his towel and pushed him into the water. I doubled over in fits of laughter as his eyes bugged out before he was submerged under the water. As he came up with my clothing, the look of trouble was written clearly across his face as I yelped and took off for the car.

Derek caught up with me before I had a chance to even put my hand on the door. He picked me up and sat me on the front hood of his car as he kissed me deeply. Playfulness aroused him even more than he was before. I didn't resist as I gave into every touch, every kiss, and every feeling he brought out of me. I let myself be lost in him, in this stranger that wanted me for me.

I quickly dried off as I felt a cool breeze come through the late-night air and slipped on the clothes he gave me.

"Thank you."

I couldn't stop myself as he was dressing himself; I smelled his cologne fragrance from his shirt. I could smell not only his cologne but Derek's musky scent. His scent drove me wild, and I could already feel myself wanting him again. Like an insatiable hunger was eating me from the inside out. Geez, I was really losing it now. If he could hear my thoughts, they would definitely send him running for the hills.

Derek looked at me sympathetically as he faced me and smiled. "What if I said that I want to give you a gift? What if I said that I could give you freedom from your immune disease... that you would no longer have to suffer?" he inquired.

Once again his gaze was intense as we sat inches apart from one another, but I couldn't suppress the nervousness that now clawed at my stomach. It was an offer any normal gal would take off screaming for help but I was intrigued. I slapped myself mentally, have I lost my mind?! I barely knew this man, and besides... he didn't mean it, maybe he was testing me.

So I did what any sane person would do in my situation, I laughed, and not just a giggle, but a full-on snorting laugh.

"I would say that you sound crazy," but I shut my mouth quickly as I realized that Derek wasn't laughing at all but had a very serious look on his face.

I quietly started backing away from him, unsure of the moment. What had I gotten myself into? What was I thinking? Was he going to kill me? Was he going to kidnap me? This is what I get for being wild and carefree. "Derek, you're kind of scaring me. Please tell me you're not a psychopath," I pleaded. "You're really cute and I would hate to have to actually hurt you. I just... I just don't do crazy."

He chuckled as he leaned back and sat on the trunk of his car. "I'm not crazy. I feel this pull towards you but it's really hard to explain. How do you feel right now? Is your neck okay? Did I hurt you?"

I shrugged, "Besides being a little scared and confused at the moment. I feel great, actually. My neck is a tad bit sore, but you did bite me, so I figure I'll have a nice hickey I'm going to have to hide. Why?"

"There's something I need to tell you. I am not a normal human," he started, but I laughed at what he said. I felt like my mind was being ripped apart but a little sliver of hope bloomed within. Maybe he's not a nut job? Maybe that's why I felt drawn to him so much when I met him? I shook my head clearing my thoughts.

"Normal human, huh?" Don't tell me you're secretly a geek that reads too many comics.

Derek shook his head, "I'm glad you can joke about this, because it's true. I'm a Lycan. Do you know what that is?"

I laughed hysterically, "Of course, the first guy I'm really interested in and want more than anything in the world, and he thinks he's a werewolf. I think you better take me home, Derek. I just can't do this level of insanity with someone."

"Kristen, stop. Please don't freak out," he pleaded.

"Derek, do you know how insane you sound?!"

"Yes! Yes, I do! But it's true. I can't stand the thought of all you've been through with no one but your best friend. Here look," he said as he grabbed my face and forced me to look him in the eyes.

The beautiful onyx was replaced by a glowing amber color. I gasped in shock, "I wasn't seeing things at the bar! Your eyes *did* change."

Derek's body tensed at my confession. Pinching the bridge of his nose, he let out a breath I didn't realize he had been holding. "Yes, let's just say, when he got close to getting physical, my beast was not happy. It took every ounce of control to keep him contained. Which is weird and rare. I've been in control of my inner beast since I was a teenager, but something about you made him almost show the entire town my family's secret."

Wait a minute, the thought began to dawn on me. He bit me while we had sex... He's a werewolf, a shifter or whatever they're called these days. Does that mean... That I would...

I figured I would try to reason with him on his level. "How do you know this will happen? Do you bite a lot of girls in distress?" I said accusingly.

I didn't have time to wait for an answer as an unbearable pain shot from my neck through my body. I doubled over and screamed.

"Derek, what is happening to me? What did you do to me!" I cried.

"It's the change, let me help you through it. The first one is always the hardest," he said as he stripped his clothes off again.

He quickly undressed me, but I couldn't even register that over the pain I was feeling. My bones popped and cracked in awkward positions, but Derek never left my side as he guided me step by step through the process.

It wasn't just the physical pain that was bad, but the mental pain that was far worse. My head felt like it was splitting in two as my consciousness gained a more vibrant voice. No, that wasn't quite right. I was no longer alone inside my mind as my soul was awakened inside, living through me as me, yet as another all-in-one.

But the fear kept me suspended in mid-transformation. The pain was surreal and surpassed anything I had gone through with Lupus. What would happen if I went through with it all the way? Would the wolf completely take over? Would I lose myself, and the person I am? Or would I be reborn into a different version of myself?

"Let go, Kristen, I promise you. It's better if you let the beast just take over." As if sensing the fear and inner turmoil within me, he gently said, "You'll still be you, Kristen, just a new you."

With a final scream, it was done. In the brightness of the full moon, I was not human anymore.

I gazed up at the full moon and howled. In it, you could hear every emotion that rolled through me. There was pain, joy, and happiness in the sound, so I howled again. I looked behind me as Derek transformed from the tall handsome stranger into a black wolf.

I noticed that we were bigger than normal wolves. Derek's eyes glowed amber in the dark, making him even more enchanting than before. I felt none of the pain from the transformation, like a bad distant memory. *I've heard birthing a child was the same way.* I thought randomly.

"*Can you hear me, Kristen?*" he asked me, pulling my attention back to him.

"*Yes, I can. Are we talking telepathically?*" I said shocked.

In my head, I could hear him chuckle. "*Something like that... How do you feel? Focus on your senses.*"

I focused on my eyes first. I could see everything in the dark so clearly as if it was still early evening, right before the sun had fully set. I tilted my head, listening all around me. It was as if someone turned up the volume on nature, the crickets and frogs were louder than before. I could hear fish jumping in the water, but they sounded like they were right in front of me. I inhaled deeply; it felt like I was smelling for the first time ever in my existence. I was amazed and completely speechless in the moment. Walking in a circle, getting a feel for my beast's body. I stalked to the water's edge and glanced at my reflection. My eyes glowed amber like Derek's eyes, but my fur was a beautiful brindle color. I tasted the water and a growl from behind me startled me. Derek stood watching me curiously with a lust filled gaze.

"*I can see, hear, smell, and taste so much more... Clearly? Is that the right word for it all? It's like I am experiencing the world for the very first time!*"

"It's not always so painful when you change, and it doesn't have to be under a full moon either, although the pull is much stronger then."

"Why me, Derek? Why change me? I believe you're a good guy, but you didn't change me because of my health issues. Even if you did feel sorry for me."

It was surreal, I still couldn't quite wrap my head around it all. The fear I felt before, trying to stop the unstoppable transformation made me feel silly, and now all I could think about was the feeling of exhilaration. I felt amazing, I couldn't bring one memory forward that I could recollect of me ever feeling this good in my entire life.

I felt like a new being... I was no longer human but inhuman. How do you explain a miraculous recovery from Lupus in a small town such as Llano? People talk a lot...especially in small towns. Plus, we don't have wolves lurking in the countryside. Coyotes, yes. Wolves, no. What would happen now because of this new transformation?

I could feel that neither of us had thought this through, but I just didn't care now. I would think about it later, for now, one thing at a time.

"Change back," he commanded. His tone wasn't harsh, but his voice carried an authority I couldn't refuse.

Instinctively, my body reacted, and the change came over me, easier and faster than before. I still wailed in pain as the bones cracked and broke, but relief was instant as my body healed itself within seconds. I could see Derek wincing at my pain every time I cried out. Briefly, I wondered if my new pain caused him pain too... Interesting, I mulled over in my head as it slightly distracted me from the bit of physical pain I was feeling.

I looked up to see Derek standing there in the moonlight in all his glory. He smiled at me, "It gets easier the more you shift."

"I hope so, although it wasn't as bad the second time around." I stood unashamed, naked in front of him.

I *felt* changed. Little things that bothered me before like being naked, didn't now and it was weird. I felt like a stranger to myself. I looked my body over, surprised to see that my scars were now gone, my body had healed itself in more ways than one.

Derek's eyes held a guilty look in them as if he was saying something. What could he possibly be hiding from me, though?

"Derek, is everything okay? You look almost worried?" I asked, feeling worried myself. Maybe he was regretting what he had done to me, for which there was no way to undo it.

"Nothing. Everything is fine," he said as his hand reached out and his thumb brushed across my cheek.

I watched his face change. Yup, he was hiding something, for sure. I would get the truth out of him no matter what though, I promised to myself.

"Derek, I will get to the bottom of it one way or the other, so don't even try holding back anything. Tell me what's on your mind," I said boldly as I squared my shoulder's back and lifted my chin.

"Kristen, you can't stay here," he confessed.

"Wait, what? What do you mean I can't stay here? This is my home! You might have changed me, but you can't make me leave!" I accused.

"I can, but I won't force you. You won't fit in with the folks here anymore. You're different now. Your wolf will crave the pack life; I know it will be an adjustment though," I turned away, angry at him.

My heart ripped in two at the harsh reality of the situation I now faced. The thoughts of leaving the only family I have ever known and loved left me feeling devastated. I couldn't leave Uncle Joe, or Samantha, or my home. Tears threatened to escape but I refused to bow down to something I never asked for from him or his authority he thought he could hold over my life.

"Derek, I can't just leave everything and everyone I have ever known and loved because you 'graciously' decided on your own, without my consent, to change me into a supernatural being! I didn't ask for this!" I yelled at him.

My eyes shifted to that of my wolf's eyes as the anger rose within. My new protective side refused to be victimized anymore. I was tired of being told what I had to do as if I had no choice in the matter. Now, as a new being, I did have a choice and I would not submit to him.

"It's also not safe. If some hunter saw you running around in wolf form, he would shoot you. You're a Texas girl, born and raised. You know I'm right. In Colorado, on pack land, we're all safe," he explained calmly as I paced around in the dark.

I could see the hurt in his eyes, this was obviously not how he thought this would go. Yet, he remained ever patient, never raising his voice at me.

"I want to go home *now*. Please. Just take me home," I pleaded. I was on the verge of tears and I didn't want to cry, crying was for the weak.

I reached for the discharged clothing and quickly dressed myself, as did Derek. He reached for my hands but I turned away and went for the passenger side of the car. As I reached for the door, he stepped in between the door and me. Derek gently grabbed my shoulders and rubbed them comfortingly.

"Kristen, I know you didn't ask for this directly, but you did without saying a word. Your story said it all. The pain you have suffered your whole life, the scars on your body, and your warrior attitude and perseverance. You smile through it, knowing that it's probably going to literally be the death of you. But now... now you can actually live, Kristen! You can experience life like never before!" he appealed to me, but I wouldn't look him in the eyes.

I needed time. I needed to think. This was happening way too fast and I just couldn't wrap my brain around it. When Derek realized that I wasn't going to answer him, he stepped away and went to the driver's side and got in. The engine purred to life as I took in a different sound. The motor hummed a tune and I reveled in it with the wind as Derek drove me home.

I just let myself be lost in thought. What would I do? Can I tell Samantha? Will I never be allowed to see my family again? Is it like a cult compound in Colorado? I could feel myself trying to rationalize everything and at the same time numb myself from the rollercoaster of emotions that threaten to run through me.

As he pulled up to my house, I was hopping out of the car before it had even stopped. I heard the other door open and Derek was hot on my heels behind me.

My heart pounded in my chest, part of me wanted Derek to steal me away. The bizarre thought hit me out of nowhere. I wanted this man, I wanted to leave with him but the other part of me wanted the safety of the known. I didn't want to leave everything and everyone I love behind.

Derek stopped on the top steps of my porch. He didn't try to stop me as I unlocked the doors to go inside without looking back.

"Kristen, I'm not going anywhere. I'll be here till you're ready to make a decision. I'll be at the Dabb's Hotel by the bridge, room nine."

"Yeah, I know the place. Don't hold your breath because I'm not going," I pouted.

"Just think about it, Kristen. That's all I ask," he implored.

"Okay," I said as I shut the door. I locked the door and rested my back against the wall. I slid down the wood in defeat as Derek's words replayed over and over again in my head. I cracked. The tears started rolling down my cheeks and the sobs came. *Ugh... I hate when I ugly cry*, I thought to myself.

For the first time in my entire life, I truly felt hopeless by the situation. At least I knew when I died, I had the eternal promise of Heaven in the afterlife. Now, what would I lose? Even though Samantha and Uncle Joe had always been there my entire life, I think this would be the straw that broke the camel's back for sure.

How would others treat me if I did go to Colorado and lived on pack land? Would they accept me, or would they try and run me out of town? More tears washed down my cheek at the sadness that threatened to eat me alive.

I forced myself to the comfort of my hidey-hole of a nook in my room and opened my laptop. At first, I pulled up all the pictures I had in my files of Samantha and Uncle Joe, the memories we had made throughout my whole life with them. I wept bitterly at the thought of letting them go and never seeing them again. Maybe I should just run away without another word or notice? No, Samantha would have the FBI tracking me down and home by dinner time tomorrow. What should I do? The ticking of the clock on the wall ate at the seconds pressing me to decide.

I decided to shift my thoughts and for hours, I researched werewolves and shifters, but most sites were bogus and just junk sites.

I paused on one site that talked about mates. My mouth dropped when I read the information, my eyes glued to the screen. Apparently, when a shifter bites the person they're intimate with, in the middle of doing the do, that marks them as mates. It only happens when a shifter's animal finds its soul mate. The shifter can't help it, as their instincts take over and mark the mate, before someone tries from a rogue pack, especially if the shifter is an Alpha. Mates are soul mates and you only meet one in your life. Being mates means that it's a forever bond, imprinted onto each other's soul and only belonging with that shifter.

My jaw dropped at the realization of the entire situation. Even if I thought it was permanent, what happened between us was literally no joke... But was that such a bad thing? I could still be me even if it included Derek. I can still have the things I wanted even with him in the picture. Why would anyone want to go through life alone? I have been alone for a very long time, even with Samantha and Uncle Joe around. I was still lonely. If Derek knew I was his soul mate, I wouldn't have to be alone.

I don't know how long I was surfing the web or lost in my own thoughts, but eventually there was nothing but the comfort of sleep.

Chapter 5

The morning sun was shining through my bedroom window as I sat up and stretched. When I saw the bright sun shining down on me, I squealed in fear and ran to the curtains, slamming them shut. Frantically, I checked my arms and legs for red welt marks that would eventually turn into blisters, which appear almost instantly with exposure to the sun.

I'm always teased about my vampire living habits, minus the blood drinking, that I've grown accustomed to in my life. It is how I live semi-healthy without the worst of the disease interfering with my life. You learn these little tricks to survive.

The memories of last night came flooding back and everything became very real once again. My shoulders slumped as I dragged myself to the bathroom to shower. Other than crying my eyes out, I felt pretty good, all things considered. I should be dragging after last night, my arms should be in full discoid Lupus rash flare, and the butterfly rash that appears and disappears like Houdini on my face should be like a wildfire explosion. But, as I looked in the mirror, I noticed *nothing*.

I quickly stripped down to my bra and underwear, examining my body. No lesions, my hair was thicker than yesterday, and no scars. Except the crescent shaped scar that laid between my neck and shoulder. I gripped the edge of the sink counter as panic set in. Why was I panicking? This is a good thing? No, it wasn't. Now I was Derek's puppet to be controlled. He wouldn't do that. Hell, I don't know anything about him. Well yeah, I did. He told me all about himself and his family last night.

"So how was your night with Mister Mysterious?!" Samantha said excitedly, bouncing into the bathroom and scaring the life out of me.

I yelped and jumped in surprise, breaking the edge of the sink off into pieces. I stared at the broken sink in shock.

The internet did say something about super strength, I mean I was no Superman, but I would be stronger than a human. *Human...* my mind pondered over again, *I wasn't human anymore.*

"Oh. My. God," Samantha said with her eyes bulging out. "Kristen are you okay? How did you..." She started as she grabbed my cut-up hands and the cuts sealed up right in front of her.

Samantha's eyes widened as both of ours met. "What? Do I have something on my face?" I laughed nervously.

Turning away from her, I looked into the mirror; my wolf's amber eyes stared back at me instead. Samantha stared at my reflection in the mirror as she turned and rushed out of the bathroom.

"Samantha, wait..." Grabbing my oversized long shirt, I ran to catch her rushing down the stairs to leave. She was in total freaked out mode, heck... I was still freaked out. "I can explain."

"Are you a vampire? Is that why you've been stuck inside all these years?!" She accused me.

"What? No!" I laughed half crazed.

"Kristen, your eyes just turned into some freaky...I don't know what, and you're just going to sit there and laugh at me like *I'm* crazy?" she said in disbelief.

"No, but I can explain," I said as I sat us down on the couch together.

"I'm listening," she said as she pursed her lips; that meant she was deciding how much of this was true and how much was bull honky.

"It happened last night..." I waited as Samantha connected the dots in her head.

"Derek! He did this to you?!" She asked, leaning in. She drew her head back as she covered her face with her hands.

"I'm still coming to terms with all this myself, Samantha," I said, patting her leg.

"Oh yeah? Seems like you're pretty cotton-pickin' calm over there, but for all I know, you're waiting to drink my blood. So, what exactly did he do to you?" She asked again.

"So, we went back-roading and ended up at The Slab. We talked about everything. I told him the truth about my illness and things ended up getting hot and heavy. One thing led to another, he bit me, and I changed," I said matter-of-factly.

She gave me a *'do you think I'm an idiot'* look as I snorted and shook my head. "*Wolf*, Samantha. I turned into a wolf because of the full moon. That is what you saw in the mirror. My wolf's eyes."

She opened her mouth, but I held up my hand, stopping her.

"I'm still learning everything, you will find out when I do. The important thing we need to discuss is that he said it's not safe for me to stay here. But Samantha... I can't leave everything and everyone I have ever known," I said helplessly.

Samantha's eyes held pity and sadness within them. "Poor Kristen, always thinking of everyone else and never herself, even though you've always needed it the most. He's right though, you can't stay here anymore, and it's not safe."

"So you want me to leave because I'm different now?" I accused, hurt by her confession.

Samantha shook her head sadly and grabbed my hand, squeezing it tightly in hers. "Kris, you are not going to lose me. I can come with you if you would like but I can't protect you from this. You're my best friend and I don't want to lose you at all. You're a part of a whole new world now, you have freedom from the disease that has held you captive your entire life," she said as a tear escaped and ran down her cheek.

The reality of her words comforted me in a new way. All I had been thinking about was everything I stood to lose, not what I stood to gain or already gained now such as freedom from Lupus.

"What do I tell Uncle Joe? He'll be heartbroken if I leave," I said, stalling.

"Tell him you were offered a job that you couldn't refuse! Oh, and that they need you right away, all expenses paid! You know Uncle Joe; he'll support you the whole way," Samantha said encouragingly.

"You'll really come with me?" I asked, chewing on my bottom lip nervously.

Samantha jokingly punched my arm, "Duh! Derek is totally hot! I wonder if any of his pack mates are just as hot?"

We giggled as I shook my head at her. She was always the boy-crazy friend but heck, we both were the same way. Lupus was always the thing holding me back and now that it was gone, I wasn't sure how to live without it.

After talking with Samantha, I could see the hope more clearly and what Derek was truly offering me other than himself. His bite offered me freedom and a new life, it offered me happiness, excitement, and adventure, to truly be the me I had always dreamed of. It might not have been the way I imagined being freed from Lupus and the dread of this life, but it was definitely something.

I heaved a deep breath as I said, "Derek is waiting at the hotel for an answer from me. He said he would wait as long as it took for me to decide."

Samantha smiled and shook her head, "He doesn't seem that bad of a man, Kristen. You've got to drop that wall sometime in life."

I nodded as she stood up and headed towards the front door, "Where are you going, Samantha?"

"Why, to pack of course, crazy! I am going the whole way with you. I will not leave you to this journey alone. Our paths are intertwined forever."

I laughed at her as I said, "I know."

But inside my heart swelled at her gesture. She, like the sister she was to me, had not forsaken me because of my newfound inhumanness. She, like always, accepted me for me and loved me endlessly. Pride and happiness was all I saw in her, encouraging me on this new journey that was about to start.

I stood in front of the door to Derek's hotel room at the Dabbs Hotel. Studying the tan paint, my insides turned at the thought of the decision...no, *choice* I was about to make. There was no going back once that door opened.

I raised my hand to knock but leaned my forehead against the door instead for a moment and braced my hands on each side of the doorframe. A noise on the other side of the door caught my attention as I tilted my head and listened intently.

Feet paced back and forth inside, and my breath caught as I heard his footsteps stop on the other side. All that separated us was a couple inches of wood, yet my heart clenched, whether in fear or hope was yet to be determined.

"Kristen, I know you're scared but I will be with you every step of the way. You're not alone. You have a new family waiting to meet you. Trust me, please. I know we barely know each other but that'll change," he whispered through the door.

My heart sped up at the sound of his voice, but butterflies fluttered up in my stomach at the sincerity of his words. Slowly, I reached for the handle, but my hand shook violently and stopped within a hair of the knob. The insecurity voices whispered inside, *what if he doesn't always want me? What if he gets tired of me in the future? What if he has changed his mind waiting for me? Why was I so nervous now?*

I laughed at myself. This man, and what he truly could be offering me, scared the crap out of me. Maybe it was too good to be true or maybe not, but frankly, I didn't give a damn. I deserved it as much as the next person... Right?

Slowly, the door crept open and Derek stood there in a low, loose-fitting pair of jeans and a black shirt. I couldn't bring my eyes to meet him, but his hand gently lifted my face as our eyes met one another's.

Tears fell down my cheeks at his gentleness, but when our eyes met, my chest began to rock with sobs. Without hesitation, Derek drew me into his chest and kicked the door shut behind me. I held onto him like an anchor and just let his touch center me.

Derek reached under my thighs and lifted me as we drifted backwards onto the side of the bed. He tucked my head under his chin and waited patiently for my sobs to stop.

When I calmed down enough, he handed me a towel to dry my face.

"Ugh... I hate it when I ugly cry," I said in a half-laugh, half-hiccup.

Derek chuckled deeply, "Oh, Kristen." He held me away from him so he could look at me. "You're just as beautiful to me."

I shoved playfully at him in a weak attempt to push him away, but Derek just laughed and held onto me tighter.

"You barely know me, I barely know you, and the stuff I was reading on the Internet, Mr. Alpha, was NOT helping!" I said dramatically.

"Oh lordy, you went online to look it up? Most of that stuff..." he started but I cut him off.

"...is a complete and total crapfest? Yeah, I know," I laughed half-heartedly.

"Kristen, please leave it to me and the pack to teach you everything. I'm not saying it's going to be easy or that there won't be challenges but we will face those challenges together, okay?"

The thought of meeting the pack, his family, made me feel nervous. I was so scared they wouldn't accept me and this would all be for nothing.

"I called my brother last night, which turned into a family discussion on the phone. My mother is overly thrilled about me having a mate but is furious with the way I changed you. There's typically a traditional way of doing things. The family rule is we can't turn our mates till after we're married and have their full consent. Honestly, the fact is that I didn't ask first and just acted selfishly. Will you forgive me?"

I nodded my head in agreement; "I do forgive you, Derek. Yes, part of you was selfish for what you did but the other part, the bigger part, had my best interest in mind. You did save me from this disease that was truly killing me from the inside out. But I guess we should talk about the other elephant in the room as well before we go on any more into this."

Derek looked at me slightly puzzled, "What other elephant?"

"The whole mate thing is exactly what I am talking about, Derek," I said, staring him down.

"Ooh... Umm..." He said blushing deeply.

I laughed at his puzzled expression as I said, "One of the sites explained about it, in fact, the mate thing was one of the few consistencies in all the sites I saw."

Derek ran a hand over his face, as he appeared to be thinking about how best to answer my question.

"Yes, that's one of the reasons I turned you, Kristen. My wolf sensed his soulmate in you. I was turning you to help cure you of your illness but the wolf in me had another plan. Do you know what being mates means?" he asked.

"Basically, it's God's version of arranged marriage for werewolves? It just hits you like a freak storm when you come across your mate and y'all bam-chicka-wow-wow while you bite the human, then y'all are bound to one another till death, or something to those standards."

Derek looked at me with his mouth agape, and then fell backwards onto the bed, laughing hysterically. "I have never heard it put that way in my entire life, but I like it."

I scooted off his lap onto the bed, laughing myself, and lay on my side facing him. "Derek, I'm scared, but you were the first person I came to after I left my house. Ever since the change, you're all I want and think about. I want the freedom you're offering and the adventure in life that waits in Colorado. But there are a few stipulations if I go with you."

Derek rolled over and took my hand in his as he said, "Anything, Kristen. I just want you to be happy. I'm just as much a slave to you as you worry about being to me but not in a bad way. I *want* to be your slave. I want to please you. I want to be near you, to touch you, make you laugh, smell your sweet fragrance, and much more. I am drawn to you in a way I have never understood," he confessed.

"How so?" I pressed, wanting to hear more.

"My parents tried to explain it to me and I have seen many of my siblings and packmates go through this. It's insane how, in a blink of an eye, you are drawn to someone but then when you become mates, you become inseparable. I thought it was all a bunch of bull, but now..." He brought my knuckles to his lips and lightly brushed them across my knuckles. "Now, I know it was all true. I have been going out of my mind about you. Waiting for you to come to me. If you hadn't shown up like you did then you would have found me at *your* front door," He chuckled, and I giggled at his confession.

"Okay, so I am a free person? I will still be able to go and do things as I want but I want to get to know you. The wolves inside us might..." I used my fingers to make air quotes. "'Love' each other and I feel it, the attraction, the want, the need, but I still don't truly know you yet. But I want to, Derek; I feel it to the core of my being that I want to," I confessed with a vulnerability that I was not used to owning up to. "I will still run my online business, I will not lose the independence I fought so hard to earn long before I met you?"

"Done. That's not a lot to ask considering everything," he smiled. "It's important to know and understand, Kristen, you're not my slave and I don't own you. We're partners and I would die protecting you from anything or anyone."

I smiled at his vow, "There's one more thing I should tell you as part of my condition to come with you."

"Oh yeah? Name it," he said slightly distracted as his fingers traced the partial opening of my shirt on the side.

"My best friend, Samantha, knows, and she's coming with me. You will help her find a reasonable job up there and she can live close by as well."

Derek's hand stilled, and I held my breath but stood my ground. He tilted his head as he thought it over in his head.

Without a moment to react, Derek yanked me onto his lap as he sat up and kissed me deeply.

"How can I refuse such requests as these? Yes, Kristen. Whatever makes you happy."

Our faces were mere inches apart and my heart thumped wildly in my chest, but I wanted this man with every fiber of my being.

"Okay, I lied. I have one more demand," I said boldly.

Derek brushed my hair back from my face, as he asked, "What?"

"Kiss me like you did last night and don't stop ever. Till the day I die, don't ever stop," My breathing was getting heavy as I waited for Derek to answer.

"Your wish is my command, my Lupie warrior, and I aim to please, ma'am."

We became a tangle of limbs and kisses in that moment and many moments more as acceptance pulled through.

Epilogue

I smiled the next day as I thought about everything. In less than forty-eight hours, my whole world had changed.

Derek helped Samantha load the last of our stuff in the U-haul. Many things were being left behind. I would not give up my home so I could come back and visit and stay awhile. Still, seeing what little we were taking, loaded up made my heart tug at my heart's strings.

His brother, Dexter, flew down within hours without question and helped with everything. Dexter and Samantha seemed very cozy already with one another as they were driving in her VW Beetle truck, and I with Derek in his mustang.

While I gained a partner for life that I still didn't understand fully, I gained so much more as a shifter. Now I know confidence and what it was like to feel good as a person. I can wake up every morning ready to face the day and take on the world and new challenges. I'd once hated myself and my life more than anything else in the world because Lupus ruled over it and dictated my every move.

Whether it was what I did or what I ate, now I know a freedom in those choices that I had never known before. Now I could enjoy the beautiful sunlight of the day, I can now revel in the night as a wolf. I am a prisoner that was set free and I will live everyday with gratitude.

I laughed at the thought of just a few days ago my body was killing itself and today I am reborn as a new person, with a whole new world ahead of me.

I am...

The Lupie Warrior.

The End

About the Author

I'm a Native Texan, born and raised close to the heart of the great Lone Star state. I was born in January of 89' and was able to grow up during a great time. I honestly don't consider myself a Millennial, and really hate that title. Also I'm a part-time working secretary and a full-time mother/housewife, as well as a Lupus Warrior.

Having Lupus, means a life of inside living, and the sun is known as my arch-nemesis, my personal kryptonite. I wanted to leave a legacy behind, something my kids could one day look back on and say, "Yeah, my mom did that."

Thanks to the encouragement of friends and family, I found a passion in writing paranormal romance books. Anything fantasy usually suits my novels and I tend to be able to reach a large audience in multiple genres. Most of my story ideas come to me in the most unexpected times and places, such as my dreams. They will plague me non-stop until I get my rear up and write it out.

I like to explore new types of characters such as Sandmen and Boogeymen for example. I really wanted to give them their own world, such as A Sandman's Forbidden Love.

God has granted me success that I never imagined was possible., which lead me to my obsession with the paranormal. Now, I know shifters aren't real but Angels are another story. So Angels are also a part of my obsession, I will sit on the computer doing extensive research on both Sandmen and Angels trying to get my facts straight.

Then, on the side, I create Art Journals that can be cross generational from thirteen to sixty years young My goal, with these types of books, is to reach people who need that extra feel good in their lives.

Connect with Author Kristen Collins:

Facebook:
https://www.facebook.com/AuthorKristenCollins/

Twitter:
https://twitter.com/Author_KCollins/

Goodreads:
https://www.goodreads.com/author/show/15424111.Tory_Kristen_Collins/

Amazon Page:
https://www.amazon.com/-/e/B01MXWRH6K/

Author Website:
http://tksky7210.wixsite.com/readnamongstheclouds/

Books by Kristen Collins

Hybrid Love Anthology:
A Sandman's Forbidden Love (**Standalone)**
Grimm Love
The Child with Silver Eyes
Throne of Storms & Ashes

Untold Series Novelette:
Eve Untold
Ruth Untold

Elsewhere Series:
Down The Rabbit Hole
Goldilocks

The Follow Art Journal Series:
Follow Your Heart and Free Your Mind
Follow the Path & Free Your Soul

Other Stories by the Author:
The Lupie Warrior
The Case of the Lost Christmas

Available on Amazon:
https://www.amazon.com/-/e/B01MXWRH6

Made in the USA
Middletown, DE
06 April 2021